||||| ||| |||| || ||| || | ||||| ||| | | || ||| || ||||
✍ **W9-AXH-339**

OLIVIA™

Builds a House

adapted by Maggie Testa
based on the screenplay "Little Big House" written by Jule Selbo
illustrated by Shane L. Johnson

Ready-to-Read

🐰

Simon Spotlight
New York   London   Toronto   Sydney   New Delhi

Craven-Pamlico-Carteret
Regional Library

Based on the TV series *OLIVIA*™ as seen on Nickelodeon™

SIMON SPOTLIGHT
An imprint of Simon & Schuster Children's Publishing Division
1230 Avenue of the Americas, New York, New York 10020
OLIVIA™ Ian Falconer Ink Unlimited, Inc. and
© 2012 Ian Falconer and Classic Media, LLC
All rights reserved, including the right of reproduction in whole or in part in any form.
SIMON SPOTLIGHT, READY-TO-READ, and colophon are registered trademarks of Simon & Schuster, Inc.
For information about special discounts for bulk purchases, please contact Simon & Schuster Special Sales at
1-866-506-1949 or business@simonandschuster.com.
Manufactured in the United States of America 0712 LAK
First Edition
1 2 3 4 5 6 7 8 9 10
ISBN 978-1-4424-5322-7 (pbk)
ISBN 978-1-4424-5323-4 (hc)
ISBN 978-1-4424-5324-1 (eBook)

This is Olivia.
And this is her father.
Father builds houses.
That is his job.

Before Father builds a house, he makes a model of it.

Olivia likes to help
build the model houses.

Father has a new client,
Mrs. Hickory.
She wants to see this model
house.

But first Father
has to pick her up
from the airport.
Olivia will keep
the model safe
while he is gone.

Olivia is happy to help!

Edwin, no!

Perry, no!

Olivia needs to find
a safer spot
for the model house.

"No one can come
into the living room!"
says Olivia.
"I must keep the model
house safe."

"Perry, no!" cries Ian.
But it is too late.

"This is not good,"
says Olivia.

"What can we do?" asks Ian.

Olivia knows what to do!
They can put the model
together again.

"All done!" says Olivia.
But something is not right.
"This does not look like a
house," says Ian.

Olivia knows what to do!
They will build a new
model house.

This one will be bigger
and fancier and redder.

"It just needs one more thing!" says Olivia.

"There," she says.

"It is perfectly perfect."

"Just in time," says Ian.

"Father is home!"

Mrs. Hickory looks at
the model house.
"How did you know that red
is my favorite color?"
she asks Olivia.

"Simple," replies Olivia.
"It is everyone's favorite
color."
Mrs. Hickory turns to Father.
"You are hired!" she says.

Later, Father tucks Olivia
into bed.
"Your model was amazing!
Thank you for all your help.
Good night, Olivia!"